THE BIG HOUSE

THE
STRIKE

A Victorian Adventure

Written and illustrated by

George Buchanan

W
FRANKLIN WATTS
LONDON•SYDNEY

THE BIG HOUSE

Summer 1859

If you leave the bustling town of Staddon and walk carefully down the track from the common you'll see the small village of Dalcombe, clustered in a steep valley. Stop and look into the distance, where the woods meet the patchwork of fields. You can just glimpse the Big House, Dalcombe Manor.

Mr Edward de Ray lives there with his granddaughter, Charlotte. Charlotte's father Jack, Mr Edward's son, comes to visit them from London from time to time.

Mrs Duff, the cook, lives there too. Her little flat overlooks the orchard. Vincent, the stableboy, occupies a small attic room, and Meg and Mary, the maids, share another.

The houseboys, Albert and Fergus, have the middle room. The window is cracked. I think Fergus broke it – up to mischief as usual!

All the staff are working at the moment. It's a typical day at the Big House...

CONTENTS

CHAPTER ONE
The Trouble Begins

Balancing the tray carefully, Vincent opened the dining room door. Mr Edward de Ray, master of Dalcombe Manor, looked up from his morning newspaper.

'Ah, coffee. Perfect timing, Vincent,' he said. He leant forward as he spoke, and stabbed the newspaper with his finger.

'Tell me, Vincent. This building workers' leader, Mr Steele. It says here that he comes from Staddon.' He paused. 'Steele. That's your name. Are you related?'

Vincent poured the coffee. 'He's my father, Sir. The building workers elected him in July. Would you like some toast, Sir?'

'No, just coffee, thank you. He's quite a troublemaker your father, isn't he?' Mr de Ray tapped the newspaper again. 'I read here that he's encouraging his builder friends to fight for a nine-hour day rather than a twelve-hour day.'

Mr de Ray looked up, smiling. 'May I give you a friendly warning, Vincent?'

'Sir?' Vincent's voice quavered.

'My son Jack is coming home on Friday. You know he manages the De Ray Construction Company for me, don't you?'

'Yes Sir, my father works for Mr Jack at De Ray's, Sir.'

Mr Edward could see Vincent's hand trembling as he poured the coffee.

'Let me give you this friendly warning then, Vincent. Keep your head down while he's here. Work in the stables as usual. Help Mr Portbury with the carts, anything really. Just keep out of Mr Jack's way. He's very angry at the moment. And if he finds out that your father is behind all this nonsense, I don't know what will happen!'

'So, I'm not to serve at the table, Sir?'

'No, Mr Trowel, my footman, should be fully recovered and back to work by then.'

'Yes Sir, he did say he was feeling much better,' said Vincent, with relief.

Mr Edward sighed deeply, sipped his coffee and turned back to his newspaper. His son's visit was going to be difficult for everyone.

***

In Railway Road, Staddon, a cluster of angry men jostled in front of the locked gates of the De Ray Construction Company.

'Why hasn't anybody opened the gates this morning?' they asked each other.

'Look! They've fitted new padlocks!'

'Open the gates, open the gates!'

One man began to kick the heavy gates.

Others pulled themselves up to look into the yard. It was deserted.

'Here comes Mr Steele,' someone shouted.

'Stop kicking the gates, Badger! Let's see what Mr Steele has to say!'

Badger stood back, and Mr Steele and his two companions stopped and faced the crowd of men.

'Men, the managers have locked us out! They're shutting us out for a week to teach us a lesson for making unreasonable demands.' He paused and saw the shock on the men's faces.

Mr Steele went on quietly, 'This is all
because we have asked our employers to cut our
working day from twelve hours to nine hours.

'Rather than talk to us, rather than negotiate,
Mr Jack de Ray and the rest of the managers
have decided to lock us out to force us to give in.
No work – no pay! That's what this means!'

He paused again and looked round at the
men. Then, punching the air, he shouted loudly,
'What shall we do? Shall we give up our demands
for a nine-hour day and shuffle back to work

with our heads down, or shall we come back at them with a strike?'

'We strike, Mr Steele. Strike! Strike! Strike!' the men yelled in unison and clapped each other on the back.

Badger, red-faced and sweating, came lurching to the front of the crowd. 'Shall we kick down the gates then, Sir?' he asked with a wild gleam in his eye.

'No, no,' said Mr Steele decisively. 'No violence, Badger. No damage. We conduct this strike as gentlemen, do you understand?'

'What about setting fire to the timber yard then, Sir?'

'No! Definitely not,' Mr Steele said wearily. Then he shouted. 'Men! The strike committee meeting will be held in the upstairs room at the Mason's Arms.

'Tell your friends we will be doling out strike pay to every worker, each Saturday. It won't be much, but it will be enough to buy food for your families.

'Anyone who wants to join the strike committee, please report to the Mason's Arms this afternoon.'

CHAPTER TWO
An Unwelcome Visitor

Back at Dalcombe Manor, the servants had
been working hard all week to prepare Mr Jack
de Ray's rooms.

Dust sheets had been folded away, his
massive mahogany bed was airing, and the
furniture had been polished.

It was Friday and Mr Jack was expected to

arrive on the evening train from London.

In the kitchen, Mrs Duff, the cook, caught Fergus by the collar and spun him round.

'A scuttle of coal for Mr de Ray's sitting room please, Fergus. And there'll be no more of my cake until his rooms are ready!'

Fergus wondered if it was always this busy when Mr Jack came home. He pounded down the cellar steps swinging the empty scuttle, ducked under a low arch and grabbed the coal trolley.

He gave it a push and jumped aboard as the little cart began to trundle along on its narrow iron rails: under the kitchen, under the cobbled yard, under the stables and into the coal cellar.

It ground to a halt by a mountain of coal.

Fergus took a shovel and quickly filled the coal scuttle. He could hear Vincent in the stable room above, humming to himself as he oiled the leather harness straps.

'Vincent,' he sang out, 'give me a push, please!'

A face appeared at the top of the steps.

'What's that, Fergus?'

'A push please, Vincent!' Fergus called again, crouching on the front of the trolley.

Vincent came down the steps. 'Just my luck, isn't it?' he said. 'Mr Portbury's ill and has had to go home. So I've got to fetch Mr Jack from the station tonight, despite what Mr Edward said about keeping out of his way.'

'Don't worry. I'll come with you,' offered Fergus. 'Give me a shove will you? What time will you leave for Staddon?'

Vincent gave the trolley a fierce push.

'Eight o'clock!' his voice echoed down the tunnel as the little trolley hurtled off.

Vincent turned and walked back up to the tack room. He'd better polish the new coachlamps before tonight too, he thought.

***

On his way upstairs with the coal, Fergus poked his head through the schoolroom door. Miss Charlotte was sitting at her desk doodling on her notebook.

'Hello, Fergus! I've nearly finished my French. Can you come out to play?' she whispered.

'Silence Charlotte! Who are you talking to?' asked Miss Franks.

Charlotte giggled and turned round to face her governess.

Miss Franks scowled. 'What's so funny, Charlotte?'

'You said silence, Miss! How can I answer if I can't talk?' she smirked.

Fergus muffled a laugh and Miss Franks spotted him at the door. 'Get out!' she yelled, jumping to her feet.

Miss Franks didn't like Fergus. He was far too cheeky for his own good and was always hanging around Miss Charlotte.

Charlotte had to be protected from people like Fergus. She was Charlotte de Ray, Edward de Ray's granddaughter, and it wouldn't do for her to mix with riff-raff like Fergus Donovan.

Charlotte giggled again. 'Go away, Fergus, or Miss Franks will explode in a minute! I'll see you later.'

Fergus dashed upstairs with the coal scuttle, into Mr Jack de Ray's sitting room.

Albert, another houseboy, was sitting on the bedroom floor, munching an apple that he had taken from the table.

'Hey Albert,' whispered Fergus, 'leave them apples alone!'

'They don't count them, you know,' giggled Albert, reaching for another and stuffing it into his pocket.

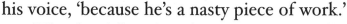

'I get the feeling that people don't like Mr Jack much. I wonder why that is?' pondered Fergus.

'They don't like him...' Albert paused dramatically and lowered his voice, 'because he's a nasty piece of work.'

'Thanks, Albert,' said Fergus sarcastically, 'that explains everything!'

'Well, you know what I mean! If he wasn't nasty, people would like him. Stands to reason, stupid. Anyway, come on, we've still got to polish his boots and light the fires.'

'Haven't we got time to play with Charlotte?' pleaded Fergus.

'Not a chance!' replied Albert.

CHAPTER THREE
Mr Jack de Ray

It was midnight when Vincent drove the carriage carrying Mr Jack into the Dalcombe courtyard. The coach came to a halt and Mr Jack de Ray jumped to the ground.

'Take my bags and run inside,' he shouted to Fergus. 'I want a private word with young Steele here.'

Fergus lifted out the heavy bags, and staggered to the back door.

Vincent bit his lip. 'Yes, Mr Jack?' he mumbled.

'Vincent,' whispered Jack maliciously, 'I suppose you know very well who is organising the strike at my building works?'

'He was elected, Mr Jack, by the men...' Vincent began.

'Don't play games with me!' Mr Jack shrieked, tobacco spit spraying into Vincent's face. He leant forward and prodded Vincent.

'It's people like your father, Vincent Steele, who are trying to ruin my business.

'If this strike of your father's continues it'll cause me no end of trouble, but I'll make sure it's even worse for you and your family.

'Ruin and disgrace, I promise you that, unless you do something about it now!' Jack de Ray whirled off, leaving Vincent shaking helplessly.

Fergus emerged from the shadows.

'That was a bit rough, Vincent,' he said quietly. 'Shall I help you put the horses away?'

***

A week later Vincent and Fergus were sitting together on the courtyard wall, eating lunch and enjoying the warm sunshine.

They watched as Meg, one of the laundry girls, ran towards them waving a scrap of paper.

'Meg's pretty isn't she?' said Fergus, grinning. 'Everyone's saying you're sweethearts!' he ventured and turned round in time to see Vincent blush bright scarlet.

'Vincent, I've got a message for you from Mr Jack!' Meg cried.

Vincent had turned white and his hands shook as he unfolded the letter Meg handed him. 'Mr Jack's been nosing around the stables, asking if I've spoken to my father about putting an end to the strike,' he said. 'He's even started to threaten me!'

'Give it here, I'll read it for you,' Fergus offered.

Vincent passed the letter to Fergus. Fergus had lived in the refuge in Staddon for a while and, during his time there, had gone to the Ragged School to learn to read.

Vincent had never been to school at all and took great pains to hide the fact.

Fergus read the letter aloud:

Dear Vincent,
Take the best carriage and go to Staddon
station to meet a Mr George, travelling first
class from Paddington. He'll be arriving on
the late train at 9.30 this evening. Leave
after lunch and make sure you speak to your
father on the way! Go alone.
Jack de Ray

'He just won't leave off, will he?' groaned Vincent, hiding his face in his hands. 'He thinks I can persuade Dad to stop the strike. There's no way Dad will listen to me!'

'Will you try?' asked Meg quietly.

'Can't hurt to try, I suppose. That's all I can do,' said Vincent. 'I'm only going to tell him that Mr Jack wants him to stop the strike.

'I won't say anything about the threats. That would make Dad really angry and things would be even worse!'

'Vincent, don't be stupid! Don't you see? If you go once, Mr Jack'll be on at you to go again and he might do all sorts of things if he thinks you can influence your father.

'Tell Mr Jack that your dad's in London for a meeting, or something!' Meg eyes filled with tears.

'What meeting?' asked Vincent wretchedly.

'Any meeting, stupid. Just make something up – say Queen Victoria is going to knight him!'

'Oh, I don't know!' said Vincent glumly.

Fergus was glad they hadn't asked for his advice. It was what Mr Edward de Ray would have called a 'dilemma'.

Instead he asked, 'Do you want me to come with you?'

'No, it says alone, remember?' said Vincent angrily as he walked away. 'I'm to go alone!'

CHAPTER FOUR
The Mason's Arms

A torn banner hung from the upstairs window of the Mason's Arms. Vincent's father's own slogan, *Nine Hours a Day to Earn our Pay*, was blazened across it.

Vincent pushed his way through the crowd. The strike committee room was upstairs and a queue of strikers shuffled impatiently on the stairs as they waited for their meagre strike pay.

Vincent could just about squeeze past. He felt awkward wearing his rich coachman's uniform when everyone around him looked so shabby.

As Vincent hurried up the wooden stairs, the men jostled and jeered loudly.

'Make way for the enemy!'

'De Ray's man coming up!'

'Excuse me,' said Vincent nervously, trying to wriggle through, 'I'm looking for my dad.'

A dirty-looking young man by the name of Nicks stepped forward, and caught Vincent by the sleeve.

'Oi, you!' he sneered.

'Let go of me!' Vincent squealed.

'Leave him alone,' someone boomed. A burly strike official recognised Vincent and elbowed his way to the top of the stairs.

'Come along Vincent, your dad's up here.' He turned to Nicks. 'We don't want your sort around here. Push off!'

He turned and took Vincent's arm and led him through the door.

'Thanks,' gasped Vincent, 'who was that?'

'He's called Nicks. A real rogue. Don't know what he was doing here!'

Vincent's father was standing behind a long table. In front of him a clerk was doling out strike pay, while another recorded the payments in a large book.

The next man in the queue approached and took off his cap.

'William Rees. Carpenter. Number ten, Railway Cottages,' he announced.

Then he burst out, 'My wife, Sir, she's just had another baby. Could the Union see its way to helping with the midwife's bills?'

He looked down at his strike pay. 'Three and sixpence won't get us very far. We're broke. Can't we go back to work yet, Sir?' he pleaded.

The men in the queue joined in, stamping their feet on the floor.

'Yeah, back to work! Back to work!'

Mr Steele strode over and held up his hand. The shouting died away.

'Men,' he began, 'we've been on strike for three weeks. Every week costs us dearly, but it costs Mr de Ray over £1,000 a week in lost business.

'That's over £3,000 so far. Mr Jack will have to give in soon. Winter's coming and outside building work will stop. It will be six months before money starts to come in for him again. Hold out men. Just a few more weeks, I promise you. We're nearly there!'

Mr Steele was greeted with cheering and stamping. He looked down at Vincent who was standing next to him, and shook his head sadly.

'They won't hold out much longer, son,' he said.

'Dad,' Vincent whispered, 'Jack de Ray's on to me. He's been threatening me and shouting and he's making my life a misery.

'He's told me I've got to try to stop you striking, Dad,' he added anxiously. 'What shall I say to him?'

Mr Steele put an arm on Vincent's shoulder and led him through the door.

'If I were you, son, I'd tell him you've spoken to me and that you've done your best.

You'd better go – this is no place for you in that uniform.'

'Oh, and take care, boy!' he added as Vincent edged his way to the stairs.

'Excuse me,' muttered Vincent nervously as he worked his way down the stairs. 'Excuse me.'

Nicks stood on the stairs waiting for him, defiantly blocking his path.

'Excuse me,' muttered Vincent, again.

Nicks didn't move and Vincent looked around him in panic. Suddenly, an unseen hand gave him a push and he went flying to the bottom of the stairs.

Vincent picked himself up, brushed himself down, and pushed through the crowd of jeering men to the door.

CHAPTER FIVE
Dirty Work

Later that afternoon, Fergus and Albert lay resting in the long grass by the main gates of Dalcombe Manor.

The late afternoon sun warmed their faces and glinted on the high stone wall next to them.

The boys had been picking apples and were now lying on their backs staring up at the blue sky, enjoying the silence.

In the distance, they heard the sound of a small cart clattering down the lane towards the gate. The two boys jumped up and Fergus climbed on Albert's back to get a better look.

'Albert,' he hissed, 'it's Nicks! You know, the crook who used to make trouble for me in the refuge!'

They watched the cart rattle through the gate and disappear temporarily from sight.

Suddenly it stopped and footsteps approached from the other side of the wall.

'Afternoon, Mr Nicks.'

'Good afternoon, Mr Jack, Sir.'

Albert and Fergus looked at each other in alarm.

'So, did Vincent go, then?' asked Jack de Ray quietly.

'He did, Sir, and 'is dad made a mighty fine speech. A few more weeks more he said, and you'll be bust.'

'He didn't persuade Steele, then?'

'Not a chance, Sir. Vincent's pathetic! I've been thinking though, Sir, what we should do is set 'im up. Accuse 'im of something. Get the police involved. You know, maybe theft or something? That would put pressure on 'is dad!'

'Don't worry, I've got something in mind...' said Mr Jack in hushed tones.

The voices moved away. The two boys picked up their baskets of apples and silently made their way back to the kitchen of the big house. Mrs Duff would know what to do.

***

Ten minutes to go. Vincent had been lying in the coach at Staddon station waiting for the train to arrive for most of the afternoon. He was bruised and tired from his experience earlier in the day.

He had spoken to his father and could do no more. He hoped Jack de Ray would understand.

Two minutes to go. Vincent closed the coach door, checked the lamps and stepped into the station.

The steam train screeched to a halt. No one got out. Vincent walked along the platform, peering into the first-class compartments.

Mr George, whoever he was, was definitely not on the train.

'What a day!' he sighed and went back out to the street. A long cold drive lay ahead of him.

Vincent stopped suddenly. The coach wasn't where he'd left it!

Then he saw it. The lamps must have blown out. Vincent walked closer. No, they were missing. Someone had stolen the new coachlamps!

'That's all I need!' muttered Vincent, exasperated.

He rummaged under the seat, pulled out an old-fashioned candle lantern and slipped it onto the hook at the front of the coach.

Wearily, he gathered the reins in his hands. He'd have to go to the police and report the theft, then drive home as best he could.

CHAPTER SIX
Police!

A week later, Vincent sat huddled in the corner of the big Dalcombe kitchen.

Ever since his drive home from the station, he'd been feeling odd. Mr Jack hadn't even been surprised that Mr George hadn't arrived! The staff were sympathetic about the theft but Mr Trowel, the footman, had some worrying news.

That evening, he'd overheard Mr Jack de Ray suggesting that Vincent had allowed one of the strikers to steal the lamps while he was at the station.

'He said you'd been to the striker's headquarters, Vincent. Did you go?'

'Of course I did. Mr Jack told me to. I got thrown downstairs because of my uniform.'

'Did you tell any of the strikers you were going to the station?' continued Mr Trowel.

'Utter nonsense!' interrupted Mrs Duff. 'We've known Vincent since he was seven years old. He wouldn't do that!'

The rest of the servants sitting around the table nodded in agreement.

Mrs Duff turned and glared at Fergus and Albert. 'Isn't it about time you two boys were in bed?' she snapped.

***

Fergus blew out the candle.

'Hey, Fergus,' whispered Albert from under the bedclothes. 'Do you think Vincent stole the lamps?'

'Of course not!' said Fergus.

'I saw Mr Jack searching Vincent's tack room,' continued Albert.

'Did you? When?'

'This morning. I was up in the loft and I heard someone come into the stables.

'I knew it couldn't be Vincent or Mr Portbury because they were both out in the fields with the carts, so I had a look through the floorboards. You get a super view from up there...'

'Get on with it!' whispered Fergus.

'Anyway, I saw Mr Jack come creeping in. He looked all round, and then went to the wall and pulled out that loose brick. You know, the one where Vincent keeps his money. I think Mr

Jack put something in there.'

'Did you check after he had gone?' asked Fergus.

'Of course I didn't! I was supposed to be helping Meg and Mary with the washing. I didn't want anyone to see me!'

'Let's go and have a look!' said Fergus.

The house was quiet as the two boys crept downstairs.

'How will we get out? The doors are all locked!' whispered Albert.

'On the coal trolley.'

They tip-toed into the hallway and unbolted the cellar door. Fergus lit a candle and they made their way to the trolley.

'Sit down, I'll push,' murmured Fergus.

There was a faint rumble as the iron wheels rolled along the narrow rails.

'Keep your head down,' whispered Fergus, 'there's cobwebs everywhere!'

The trolley stopped at the coal heap. All was silent.

Quietly the two boys climbed the steps, pulled open the door into the corridor and tiptoed into the tack room.

They were in a small whitewashed room.

Coats, blankets, saddles and bridles hung from a row of iron pegs. Chests and boxes lined the floor. This was where Vincent repaired and oiled the harnesses.

'Over here! Hold up the candle,' said Albert. He stood on a chest, wobbled the loose brick free and tentatively felt inside the hole.

'Nothing there!' he announced.

'Are you sure?' said Fergus, climbing up next to Albert.

Fergus held the candle higher and Albert reached in for another look. There was something at the back of the hole. It was a white envelope!

'What is it?' asked Fergus.

'It's a lock of hair.' Albert held out a loop of auburn hair. 'It looks like Meg's!'

The two boys giggled.

'Is there anything else in there?' asked Fergus.

Albert put the envelope back and pushed his fingers to the back of the cavity. There was definitely something else in there.

It was a small red ticket!

Albert pulled it out.

'It's a pawnbroker's ticket,' whispered Fergus. 'Vincent must have taken something valuable to the pawnshop and borrowed some money. This is the ticket that proves he owns whatever it was he took there.'

Albert was mystified. 'But Fergus, it's not Vincent's. Mr Jack put it there, I'm sure he did.'

'Shh! Someone's outside!' whispered Fergus.

Suddenly they heard a door shutting and voices in the courtyard. Then a key scraped in the lock of the stable door!

'Blow out the candle!' hissed Fergus, pushing the brick back into place and shoving the ticket into his pocket.

As quick as they could, the two boys raced up the wide wooden steps to the loft and peered down through the hatch. They were just in time to see a small group of people enter the room.

'Come on, Vincent. Come along in,' said a voice. A burly policeman with a lantern was holding the door open.

'Look, Vincent's still in his nightshirt!' whispered Albert.

'So are we!' said Fergus and the two boys giggled.

'After you, Mr Jack,' said the policeman.

Jack de Ray entered the room and the Constable closed the door.

'What do you want?' Vincent cried. 'I haven't done anything!'

'We're just looking for the stolen lamps, or for anything that will help us to find them, son,' said the policeman.

'But I haven't taken them!' Vincent shouted. 'I reported them stolen the minute I left the train station!'

'I know. I'm sorry, Vincent. But we've searched your bedroom, we'll just search in here and then you can go back to bed.'

Vincent stumbled across to his stool and sat down. It looked as if he was crying.

The boys watched as Jack de Ray and the policeman lifted down the bags hanging on the walls and rummaged through them. They tried the boxes and chests on the floor and then emptied out Vincent's box of waxes, oils and cloths. Nothing.

'What about up there?' Mr Jack was pointing to the loose brick. 'Do you keep anything up there, Vincent?'

'Money, sometimes,' muttered Vincent.

'I'll hold the lantern,' offered Mr Jack.

Fergus and Albert held their breath.

Vincent jumped up. 'Don't!' he shouted. 'It's mine. It's private!'

The policeman reached in and pulled out the envelope. 'Nothing wrong here, Mr de Ray,' he called glancing into it. 'I'll put it back.'

'Are you certain?' said Mr Jack, puzzled. 'Is there nothing else in there?'

'Nothing at all,' said the policeman, reaching to the back of the hole. 'Thank you, Vincent. You can go back to bed now!'

Vincent scurried away, holding his head in his hands, sniffing loudly.

'He doesn't seem the sort of lad to steal lamps, Mr de Ray. Who did you say saw him at the pawnbrokers, Sir?' asked the policeman, puzzled.

'Someone I know, Constable. A reliable young man. Vincent has hidden that pawn ticket somewhere, you can be sure of that, and I'll find it!' Mr Jack looked confused and angry as he shut the door.

Fergus and Albert looked at each other.

'We'll give the ticket to Mrs Duff in the morning!' Fergus said. 'She'll know what to do.'

CHAPTER SEVEN
A Trip to Town

Albert and Fergus stood by the kitchen door.

'Mrs Duff? Can we talk to you for a minute?' asked Fergus.

Mrs Duff looked up from her pastry board. 'What's the matter, boys?'

'Do you promise not to tell anyone?'

'Yes, yes,' mumbled Mrs Duff.

'Well, Albert saw Mr Jack hiding this pawn ticket in Vincent's tack room,' said Fergus.

'It was yesterday, Mrs Duff. I was working in the loft,' added Albert, quickly.

'Hiding more like! If I went up there I'd most likely find the rest of my honeycakes!'

Albert looked embarrassed.

'What shall we do with it? I think it's important. The police came looking for it last night,' continued Fergus.

'How do you know?' asked Mrs Duff.

'We were there!' declared Fergus.

'But they didn't find it, because you had it?'

The two boys nodded proudly.

Mrs Duff peered at the ticket. 'I wonder what it's for?' she said. 'Alice's Yard. Where's that?'

'Staddon, Mrs Duff. I know the place,' answered Fergus eagerly. 'Shall I go and find out what the ticket's for?'

Fergus looked up at the tubby man sitting beside him in the cart.

'It's lucky you were going into Staddon anyway, Mr Portbury,' he said.

'Lucky? Mrs Duff told me I had to!' huffed Mr Portbury.

Houses crowded each side of the road. Carts and coaches jostled to get past and people thronged the pavements.

A group of strikers lounged idly on the street corner, hissing and whistling as they went by. Beggars ran up to them pleading for money.

'It's a good job Mr Jack de Ray isn't with us,' remarked Mr Portbury. 'These chaps would have a few things to say to him, I think. Now, where is this shop of yours, Fergus?'

'Down Water Lane, past the refuge and right at the end,' said Fergus. 'This is where I lived before I came to Dalcombe,' he added, looking around for familiar faces.

'Noisy around here, isn't it?' remarked Mr Portbury, as a steam train thundered across the iron bridge on its way to Bristol.

Fergus wasn't listening. He was watching out for the turning.

'Right here, Mr Portbury,' Fergus shouted and pointed to a narrow alley.

They had reached the poorest part of town. Decrepit buildings towered above them, blocking out the light.

The cobbles glistened with muck and slime and a bunch of bedraggled children followed them, calling for money.

Fergus spotted the three golden balls hanging from a horizontal bar. 'There's the shop,' he said, pointing to the sign.

Mr Portbury stopped the cart and Fergus ran inside.

He could just about see over the counter. An old man was peering into the back of a gold watch. Piled around him were pots, hats, pistols and other treasures.

Behind him were rows and rows of shelves heaped with buckets, brooms, sticks, cloaks, bottles and boxes.

This was how the poor borrowed money.

They came with anything they could sell and Mr Goodchild offered them cash in exchange for their goods. Never the full value.

If they couldn't repay, he kept their goods and sold them later. A lot of strikers had been to see him. He, at least, had done well out of the strike.

Fergus knew Mr Goodchild and the old man grinned down at him.

'I've got this ticket, Mr Goodchild. Any chance you can tell me what it's for and who brought it?' he asked.

'How did you get hold of this, Master Fergus?' he asked, peering at it. 'I gave this to Mr Nicks about two weeks ago. Did he give it to you?'

'No, Mr Goodchild, we found it. What's it for please?'

Mr Goodchild turned round and

disappeared into the gloom at the back of the shop. A moment later he reappeared and placed two shiny coachlamps on the counter.

'Well, Fergus,' he chuckled, handing him back the ticket, 'these are not much good to you, are they?'

'No, Mr Goodchild, but thank you for your help!' called Fergus, as he ran out of the door clutching the ticket.

***

'Well Fergus, what did you find?' Mrs Duff was standing by the range in the Dalcombe kitchen, adjusting a row of pheasants on an iron spit.

'The ticket is for the two lamps, Mrs Duff,' whispered Fergus. 'Mr Nicks pawned them.'

'Isn't he the young man you saw drive up and speak to Mr Jack a couple of weeks ago?'

'Yes, he must have stolen the lamps, pawned them and sent the ticket to Mr Jack.'

'Then Mr Jack must have hidden it in the tack room hoping the police would find it,' added Mrs Duff. 'I wonder what we should do?' she said to herself.

Mrs Duff looked around her and then bent

down to whisper in Fergus's ear.

'Go to the laundry, Fergus. Meg and Mary have just finished the washing. Find Mr Edward's trousers and put the ticket in his pocket.

'Don't let anyone see you do it and don't, whatever you do, put it in Mr Jack's trousers!'

Fergus ran off to the laundry. The door was open and piles of clothes were heaped on the scrubbed pine tables ready for ironing.

He went over to the pile of laundered men's trousers and picked through them. Beneath Mr Jack's checked trousers lay a pair of trousers with very long legs. Mr Edward was tall and thin, these must be his trousers!

Fergus listened. He could hear Meg chatting to Mary in the boiler room. Quickly he slipped the ticket into the trouser pocket.

CHAPTER EIGHT
A Red Ticket

The news arrived the next day. The strikers had given in and the building workers were trooping back to work.

In Staddon, everyone seemed to be celebrating. The locked gates of the builder's yard were thrown open. At last there would be work and families would have money to spend!

The building workers had given the strike their best shot but couldn't hold out any longer.

Jack de Ray was in a sunny mood.

'A perfect day for a family photograph, Father!' he said to Mr de Ray as they walked together on the lawn.

'Why don't you bring out your new camera and photograph the family and staff on the lawn?'

The news spread through the house quickly. People ran to put on their best uniforms and their smartest frocks.

Soon there was an expectant crowd milling about on the lawn. Mr de Ray was going to take a picture.

He set up his tripod and lifted the heavy camera into place.

Fergus and Albert brought out chairs for the family and arranged them on the lawn.

Mr Jack ushered the family to their seats.

'Now the staff!' he shouted and waved for them to come forward to stand with the family.

'We'll have the maids sitting on the grass at the sides. Footmen in the middle at the back!' he shouted. 'Come on, Mrs Duff! What's wrong?'

Mrs Duff was frightened. 'What about the harmful rays from the camera, Sir?' she asked.

Everyone laughed. 'The camera collects light, Mrs Duff. Nothing comes out of it to harm you,' called Mr de Ray. 'Where's Vincent? And where's Meg?' he asked.

'Vincent hasn't quite been himself since the incident with the police, Sir, and I've asked Meg to stay with him,' Mrs Duff called back.

Fergus and Albert sat together right at the front and grinned. Meg's help was just what Vincent needed to get better!

'Now,' called Mr de Ray. 'Everyone has to sit still for three seconds. Can you all manage that?'

Everyone nodded, although Mrs Duff still looked a little frightened.

'Albert,' called Mr de Ray. 'Can you do up your coat buttons like the rest of the staff, please?'

'No, Sir,' replied Albert. 'Not when I'm sitting down. It's got a bit small for me.'

Everyone chuckled.

'Quiet now!' Mr de Ray called. 'I'll hold my handkerchief up in the air. When I drop it, you can all relax. Ready?' And he pulled out his red and white spotted handkerchief.

A small red ticket floated out and landed on the grass.

Mr de Ray stooped down, picked up the ticket and peered at it.

Then he put it in his pocket. Everyone saw, but only a few people realised what it was.

He looked at his watch, lifted his hand and counted the seconds.

No one moved. The handkerchief fell and everyone began laughing and cheering.

Taking a photograph was a new and exciting experience!

***

Three days later, Fergus and Albert were outside picking apples for Mrs Duff.

They saw Mr Edward and Jack approaching. Mr Edward leaned on his cane and motioned to his son to sit down on the short grass .

The boys stopped picking the apples and hid behind a tree.

'Jack,' said the old man, 'I hear you're off to London. Before you go, will you kindly explain how this pawnbroker's ticket got in my pocket?'

'I really don't know, Father,' muttered Jack.

Suddenly Mr Edward leapt up. 'Before you continue with your lies,' he shouted. 'I should tell you that I asked Mr Portbury to collect our lamps from the pawnbrokers and Vincent is polishing them as we speak.

'And I should also mention that you were seen putting the ticket in the tack room and that you were heard talking to a petty criminal called Nicks by the front gates.'

He stopped and glared at his son. 'You weren't trying to incriminate one of my staff were you, Jack? If you were, I suggest you had better apologise both to me, and to young Vincent. And in his case you can do more than apologise. He's planning to get married. Perhaps you would like to help him in some way? You will let me know what you do, and you will do it before travelling to London tonight.'

Mr Jack went bright red and began to stammer.

Fergus and Albert crept away. It would never do to be found listening to this kind of private telling-off. As soon as they were out of earshot, they raced back to the house.

Vincent just had to hear this!

THE BIG HOUSE

NOTES

STRIKES

By 1859, it was legal to form trade unions to negotiate for increases in pay and improvement in working conditions.

In the summer of 1859, there began a building workers' strike, which affected

London and much of the country.

The trade union demanded a nine-hour day and, to make a point, the workers at one firm, Messrs Trollope and Sons, began a strike.

In retaliation, the employers locked the gates of all their building yards, hoping to force the strikers back to work.

The stalemate lasted right through the autumn into the winter, causing great hardship to the striking workers and their families.

STRIKE FUNDS

Many trade associations contributed money to the building workers' strike fund including French polishers, saddle and harness makers, umbrella makers, weavers, bookbinders, farriers, tinplate workers and glass cutters.

In August 1859, the union made weekly strike payments to skilled workers of 12 shillings (60 pence) a week. However, by December, funds were running low and three shillings and sixpence (17½ pence) was all they could afford.

PHOTOGRAPHY

Photography in Victorian times was a hobby for the very rich. A camera and developing kit would have cost about £600.

Photography was viewed with fear by many people, who suspected that the camera emitted harmful rays or vapours.

In 1829, it took nearly eight hours' exposure to take a photograph. By 1837, Louis Daguerre had reduced exposure time to 20 minutes per photograph.

Even so, having your photo taken was a gruelling business. Sitters were propped up and put in position, with their heads held in a neck brace to prevent movement.

Once a photographic plate had been exposed, it was essential to get it to the darkroom and develop it as soon as possible.

The photographer had about 10 to 15 minutes in which to take the picture and get the exposed plate back to the darkroom.